The Great Snail Race

adapted by Kim Ostrow

illustrated by Clint Bond and Andy Clark

Based on the teleplay *The Great Snail Race* by Paul Tibbitt, Kent Osborne, and Merriwether Williams

SIMON SPOTLIGHT/NICKELODEON

New York   London   Toronto   Sydney

Stephen Hillenburg

Based on the TV series *SpongeBob SquarePants*® created by Stephen Hillenburg as seen on Nickelodeon®

 SIMON SPOTLIGHT

An imprint of Simon & Schuster Children's Publishing Division

1230 Avenue of the Americas, New York, New York 10020

Manufactured in the United States of America
First Edition 10 9 8 7 6 5 4 3 2 1
ISBN 0-689-87313-1

"Well, I guess I can't enter Gary in that," said SpongeBob. "Sunday's laundry day!"

Squidward sighed. "You can't enter Gary because Gary isn't a purebred! But Snellie has papers!" he said. He shoved his fancy document toward SpongeBob.

"Hmmm . . . 'Property of Squidward Tentpoles,'" Patrick read.

"That's Tentacles!" corrected Squidward.

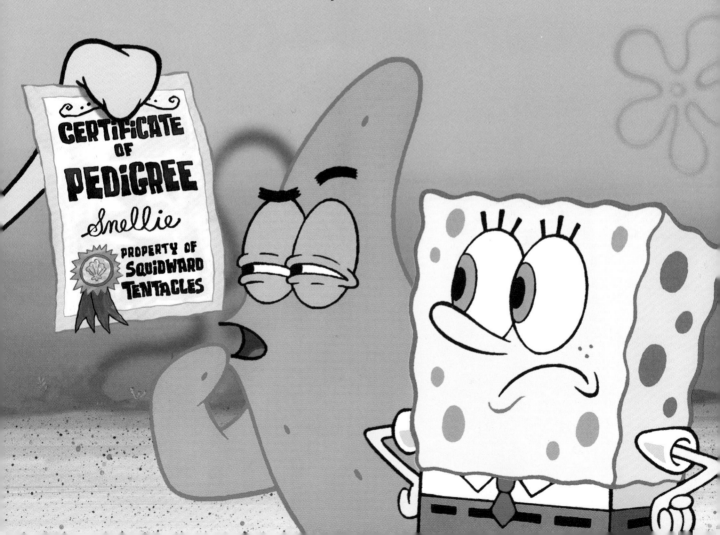

CERTIFICATE OF PEDIGREE

Snellie

PROPERTY OF SQUIDWARD TENTACLES

"Patrick, are you thinking what I'm thinking?" asked SpongeBob.

"Yeah," said Patrick. "I should get a snail and enter it in that race and beat Squidward."

"No, no, no!" shouted SpongeBob. "I'm thinking of entering Gary in that race and beating Squidward's snail."

SpongeBob had a lot of work to do to whip Gary into shape. First, he made a nutritional smoothie for his snail.

"Meow," said Gary.

"Well, of course I expect you to eat this," said SpongeBob. "It's scientifically designed to help you win tomorrow."

Gary took one look at the drink and slithered out of the room.

Patrick came over to show SpongeBob his new snail.

"Your snail is a rock," said SpongeBob.

"Yeah, I know," said Patrick proudly. "He's got nerves of steel. See you at the race!"

SpongeBob realized the competition was getting fierce.

SpongeBob blew his whistle. "Let's start with some sprints. On your mark, get set, go!"

Gary barely moved.

"Come on, Gary!" shouted SpongeBob. "You've gotta start training if you're going to win." Just then Squidward peeked in.

"Don't waste your breath, SpongeBob. That mongrel of yours doesn't have a chance," Squidward said confidently.

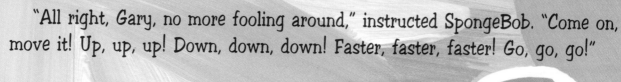

"All right, Gary, no more fooling around," instructed SpongeBob. "Come on, move it! Up, up, up! Down, down, down! Faster, faster, faster! Go, go, go!"

The day of the race finally arrived.

"Well, SpongeBob, I didn't think your mongrel mutt would even find the starting line," snickered Squidward. "Congratulations."

"Save it for the loser's circle," said SpongeBob. "Gary happens to be in the best shape of his life."

Gary coughed and wheezed.

SpongeBob gave Gary his final pep talk. "Listen up. You're the undersnail. Everybody's already counting you out. Now, get out there and win!"

"Meow," muttered Gary.

"On your mark!" shouted the referee. "Get set! Slither!"

"And they're off," said the announcer. "Number six, Snellie, rockets out of the starting box, leaving the other two competitors in the dust."

"Go, Snellie! You got it, baby!" cheered Squidward.

SpongeBob was not having the same luck. Gary hadn't budged from the starting gate.

"What are you doing, Gary?" shouted SpongeBob. "The race has started. Let's go! Start moving! You're blowing everything we trained for!"

Patrick's snail was also at the starting line. "It's okay, Rocky," Patrick said. "You go when you feel like it."

Gary slowly began to move. He panted heavily as he trudged ahead. "Not good enough!" shouted his coach. "Faster!"

The more SpongeBob yelled, the faster Gary tried to go. But it was no use. Gary was exhausted.

"That coach is pushing that snail too hard," said the announcer.

Suddenly, Gary's bloodshot eye popped like a tire!
"It looks like number seven has a blowout," said the announcer.
Shortly after, Gary's other eye blew.

"Make that two, folks," said the announcer.

"Uh . . . Gary, you can stop now," said SpongeBob.

Gary began to spin out of control—and headed straight for the wall! BAM!
The crowd gasped.

"Nooooooo!" shouted SpongeBob. "Hold on, Gary, I'm coming!"

SpongeBob raced to Gary's side.

"One of the coaches has raced onto the track. That is an automatic disqualification. Looks like number six has this race all wrapped up, ladies and gentlemen," said the announcer.

Squidward cheered. "Come on, Snellie. It's all you!"

"Oh, Gary," cried SpongeBob. "Why didn't you just say I was pushing you too hard?"

"Meow," said Gary.

"You did?" asked SpongeBob. "Oh, Gary, why didn't you tell me I wasn't listening?"

"Meow," answered Gary.

"You did? Oh, Gary!" wailed SpongeBob.

Suddenly, Squidward's prize snail stopped racing. She turned to look at Gary and then rushed to his side. The two snails looked into each other's eyes and purred.

"My oh my, folks," said the announcer. "I've never seen anything quite like it. It seems Snellie, the leader, just went back to comfort Gary."

"Looks like you and me are in-laws. Eh, Squidward?" said SpongeBob.

The crowd cheered as the winner crossed the finish line.

"But that's impossible," said Squidward. "If Snellie didn't win, then who did?"

"And the winner is," shouted the announcer, "Rocky!"

The crowd went wild! Patrick started to laugh until he cried.

Squidward moaned. "My purebred, which cost me seventeen hundred dollars, lost to a rock."

Patrick rushed to Squidward's side. "Don't worry, Squidward. I know how much you wanted to win, so I had the trophy engraved to you."

Squidward took the trophy in his tentacles. "Gosh, Patrick, thanks!" He looked at the plaque and read it out loud. "'The first-place snail racing cup presented to Squidward *Tortellini.*'"

Patrick and SpongeBob happily put their arms around their friend. "Will I ever win?" grumbled Squidward.

SQUIDWARD
TORTELLINI

It was a sunny morning in Bikini Bottom. A mailman knocked on Squidward's front door. "Aha!" said Squidward. "I can't believe it's finally here."

The mailman glanced at Squidward's signature. "Thank you, Mister . . . mmmmm . . . Tennis Balls."

"That's Tentacles!" corrected Squidward.

"Hey, check out Squidward's new snail," said Patrick.
"Looks like Gary has a new playmate," said SpongeBob.
Squidward rolled his eyes. "I wouldn't let Snellie here play
with your mongrel mutt. See? Snellie even has her own
pedigree papers. So if you'll excuse us, she has
to start her training for Bikini Bottom's
Snail Race. She'll be winning this Sunday."